Doodlebug Alley

Other titles by Robert Swindells
in the **Mammoth Read** series:

Hurricane Summer
Roger's War

Robert Swindells

Illustrated by Kim Palmer

Doodlebug Alley

Mammoth

. . . we that are young
Shall never see so much nor live so long
King Lear

For Winnie the Gunner and Norman the Fire-Fighter
RS

For all the children at Woodmancote County Primary School
KP

First published in Great Britain in 2000 by Mammoth
an imprint of Egmont Children's Books Limited,
239 Kensington High Street, London W8 6SA

Text copyright © 2000 Robert Swindells
Inside illustrations copyright © 2000 Kim Palmer
Cover illustration copyright © 2000 Peter Greenwood

The moral rights of the author, cover illustrator and illustrator have been
asserted

ISBN 0 7497 3860 X

10 9 8 7 6 5 4 3

A CIP catalogue record for this book is available from the British Library

Typeset by M Rules

Printed in Great Britain by Cox & Wyman Ltd,
Reading, Berkshire

Contents

One

Horrid things, doodlebugs. Little black aeroplanes that fly by themselves. They come buzzing over with nobody in them, and when their engine stops they fall. You don't know when the engine will stop. You see a doodlebug in the distance and you think, *Stop now and fall before you get near me*, but the engine keeps going and it gets close and then you start whispering, '*Come on, come on, keep flying, don't stop now*'. Then it's directly overhead and you hold your breath. If the engine cuts out now you're dead,

1

because the explosive in a doodlebug's nose is enough to blow up half a street. '*Go on,*' you whisper as it flies over your house, and you feel ashamed because what you're really saying is, go and fall in somebody else's street, on to somebody else's house. Go kill someone's granny but don't kill mine.

Sometimes you'll see thirty or forty in a single day, and they come at night as well, and most of them fall in somebody's street, somewhere, making orphans and widows and smoking great holes with buses sticking out.

It's the summer of 1944, I'm Sandra, and just when we thought we'd done being bombed, old Hitler goes and invents this secret weapon he calls the V1 and we call the doodlebug. And don't think this is the *first* bit of bother that man's caused me nor the second neither, 'cause it's not. Not by a long chalk. If you're not doing anything I'll tell you about it. But I'm warning you, it's not all fun and games.

Two

It began in 1939, the day war broke out. I was six and Joyce was thirteen. She's my sister. Seems the government had known war was coming and that our cities would be bombed, so they'd made this plan to save the kids. Never asked us if we *wanted* to be saved, mind. No. First thing *I* knew was when Joyce says to me, 'You'll never guess what, Sand – we're off to the country.'

'*Are* we, Joyce?' I says. 'Are we *really*?' 'Course, I thought she meant *all* of us – Mum and Dad, Joyce and me. When I

4

realised it was to be just her and me, I said, 'No. I'm not going without Mum.' Then they told me I'd no choice, it was all arranged. We were off to somewhere called Siffley, on a train with a lot of other kids.

'It's for your own good!' shouts Mum through the bathroom door. I'd locked myself in, see. She didn't understand how frightened I was. Nobody did. She threatened, pleaded, cried even, but I wouldn't unlock that door. I was still in the bathroom when Dad came home from work, and when I wouldn't open up for him, he put his shoulder to the door and broke off the lock.

Siffley was awful. Joyce and me were put to stay with a couple called Wendover, who

were so old their own daughter had grown up and left. We had her room, and the way Ma Wendover went on, you'd think it was Buckingham Palace. 'Mind Wendy's dressing table!' 'Keep your stuff off Wendy's shelves!' 'Which of you urchins tracked mud on Wendy's carpet?' Wendy Wendover. Only duffers like them would give their kid a stupid name like that. Their name for *us* was the urchins, except in company.

I won't go on about it. The Wendovers didn't even pretend to like us, the kids at the local school hated us, and the villagers stared at us on the high street as if we'd come from the moon. I cried every night for Mum, I couldn't help it, and sometimes Ma Wendover would hear me and rap on the door and shout, 'Stop that silly snivelling at once, and go to sleep!' She'd have made a good Nazi. One morning I woke up and found I'd wet the bed. *Wendy's* bed. I've never been so terrified as I was then, not even during an air raid. Joyce saw how frightened I was, and d'you know what she did? She took the blame. She did. 'It was me, Mrs Wendover. Too much Ovaltine before bed. Sorry.'

'Filthy little urchin,' Ma Wendover called her, but she was wrong. A hero's what Joyce was that morning. A war hero.

Anyway, when we'd been in Siffley eight weeks and no bombs had fallen on London, Mum came and got us. It was the happiest day of my life. The Wendovers told Mum they'd loved having us. 'We're going to miss them *terribly*,' says Ma Wendover, and bends down so I can kiss her goodbye. If she'd still mattered I'd have bitten her nose off.

Three

It was lovely to be home, to sleep in my own bed again, but being evacuated had done something to me. I didn't want to let Mum out of my sight. Thought I was going to lose her, see. 'I don't want to go to school,' I howled, that first Monday after Joyce and me came home.

'But it's St Boniface's, sweetheart – your old school. You *love* it at St Boniface's.'

'No I *don't*, I want to stay with you. Let me, Mum, *please*.'

It was no use though, I had to go. Mum

dragged me grizzling all the way, and when
we got in the yard Mrs Turpin came out and
said it was nice to have me back, even
though I *was* being very silly at the moment.
She took my hand in a firm grip and led me

up the steps, sobbing my heart out. At the top I looked back and Mum had gone. I knew I'd never see her again.

I ran home at playtime, through the gate and up the road. Wasn't supposed to of course. When I got home Mum had gone, as I'd known she would. I was shrieking at the top of my voice and battering the door with my fists when Mrs Ashcroft from next door came out. 'It's all right, dearie,' she says, cuddling me. 'Your mum's slipped up the shops, that's all. She'll be back in a jiffy, you see'f she's not.'

And of course she's right. I'm sitting in Mrs Ashcroft's window with red eyes and a biscuit and here she comes, dangling her shopping basket. We run out and I fling my arms round her and she says, 'What *you* doing home, Sand – bomb the school, did they?'

It was a joke, but a few weeks later the Germans *did* start bombing London and I got even more nervy. *What if a bomb gets Mum while I'm at school? Who'll look after me?* I suspected the Wendovers'd get the job on grounds of previous experience, which didn't help. I couldn't escape at playtimes any more because the teachers watched me like hawks. The kids thought it was no end of a joke, me wanting my mum at six and a half. Called after me all the time in the yard. *Namby-pamby, yummy-yummy, wears a nappy, sucks a dummy.*

I didn't.

The fear of losing my mum was just starting to wear off when something happened that set me right back again. Dad had been called up into the RAF not long after Joyce and me came back from Siffley and, after training, had been posted to Stranraer in Scotland. It sounded a long way away but Mum said, 'It's all right, Daddy's cooking not flying, and the Germans aren't bombing Stranraer.'

One day – it was a Saturday – Lenny Ashcroft was showing me and Joyce his shrapnel collection out front when the postman came. I ran in to see if there was a letter from Dad and there was, only I knew there must be something wrong 'cause Mum wouldn't read bits out loud like she usually did. 'Read us a bit,' I pestered, but she shook her head. 'Aw, go on, Mum, *please*.' Then I noticed tears on her cheek. I ran outside. 'Joyce,' I gulped, 'something's wrong. Mum's crying.'

Turned out Dad had met this woman in Stranraer. Canadian nurse. They'd fallen in love and he didn't think he'd be coming home next leave, and after the war he'd most likely go with her to Canada.

Being six and a half I didn't understand, but I knew Canada was even further than Scotland and I heard Mum crying at night and knew we'd lost Dad, which shows I'd been right all along. If dads can leave and never come back, so can mums. It's a matter of time, that's all.

And the time passed without us hardly
noticing, what with the Blitz and rationing
and the blackout and all that. A lot of kids
had been sent away again when the Blitz
started, but not Joyce and me. With Dad

gone, Mum needed us, and I needed her more than ever.

Anyway, things go on like this and before I know it I'm coming up to ten and Joyce is seventeen, practically grown up. The bombing has stopped, so I don't worry about Mum quite as much as I used to. Joyce has got a job in munitions and I'm glad, because it means she won't have to join the Forces. I still miss Dad of course, but Joyce is so smashing with me it's like having two mums. Then one day she comes home and says she's something to tell us, and she's *only* gone and joined the ATS. Didn't have to. Volunteered. Pleased as punch she is but *I*'m not, and neither's Mum.

But off she goes and it's just the two of us,

except when Gran hobbles round. We get used to it. After a bit a letter comes from Joyce to say she's posted to an anti-aircraft battery. She's not allowed to say where but it's a Banbury postmark. Gran says, 'She's got herself a cushy number then, seeing as how Jerry don't come over no more.'

The day after Gran says this is the day the doodlebugs start.

Four

It was quarter past eight in the morning. We'd had scrambled egg for breakfast and I was feeling sick. It was made with egg powder and it was disgusting. I'd just told Mum so, and she was snapping at me to get my blazer on, when the sirens started. We gaped at each other. Couldn't believe it. Hadn't heard a siren in months. Like Gran says, Jerry don't come over no more.

'Oh, no,' goes Mum, 'we're not starting *that* again, surely?' She grabbed my hand and we clattered down the cellar steps to the

Morrison shelter, which is like a kitchen table made of steel. You crawl under it and if your house collapses it stops you getting crushed. We sat listening. It wasn't dark because our cellar had a ground-level window and it was a bright morning. Felt cock-eyed somehow, waiting for bombs in broad daylight. Mum whispered, 'I hope your gran's taken shelter.' It's funny how it makes you talk in whispers.

Then we heard a strange noise, not like an aeroplane at all. More like a motorbike a few streets away. It got louder. Sort of popping, bubbling sound. 'Here it comes,' murmured Mum, but she hadn't a clue what sort of thing it was, only that there was something in the sky. We held our breath and clung to each other as it passed over and its noise began to recede. Then all at once it stopped. We unclinched and I looked at Mum and she shrugged as if to say, don't ask me.

A moment later a loud, flat explosion shook the cellar floor and something invisible slammed my ears as the window burst inwards, spitting splinters across the flags. I threw myself into Mum's arms and she rocked me, murmuring, 'All right, it's all right, darling, only a silly old window.'

In my half-deafened state I thought she said widow. 'Silly old widow?' I murmured and she chuckled.

'I s'pose I *am*, duck, now. Good as, anyway.' She'd a joke or two left in her then. Not like later.

Five

That was the first one. It had fallen a quarter of a mile away, in Henrietta Street. We didn't know that till next day, and seven others had gone over by then. Flying bombs we called them at first, doodlebug came later. If we'd known how many there were to be, I think Mum and I would have left London.

I dunno, there was something about them. Something that made them seem worse than ordinary bombs. See, your ordinary bomb is dropped from a plane, and somebody in the plane has decided exactly where to drop it. He's the enemy, but at least he's a human being like you. He's got a mum he might never see again. He's dangerous, but he's *in* danger too. It's him and you, if you know what I mean.

Your flying bomb . . . well it's *different*, isn't it? Nobody's there. It's automatic, like . . . like being attacked by a robot. Yeah, that's *it*. A robot. That's what a doodlebug *is*. And a robot's got no *feelings*, doesn't *know* anything. You can't scare it, hurt it, make it wish it'd stayed home with its mum. You can fill the sky with searchlights and shells till you're blue in the face, but unless you score a direct hit, it'll keep on in a dead straight line till its engine stops.

After that first day they came over in swarms, round the clock. The siren would go, you'd dash to the shelter, the all-clear would fetch you out and ten minutes later the siren would go again. For some reason, more doodlebugs were falling on our bit of London than anywhere else and people started calling it Doodlebug Alley. After a while they stopped using the sirens, not just in our district but all over London. Well, it was getting to be every few minutes and people had things to do. You couldn't keep bobbing in and out of your shelter all day like a flipping jack-in-the-box. You'd hear that throbbing noise and either ignore it or throw yourself flat. I usually threw myself flat.

They closed the school, though, and I wasn't half glad. I mean *all* the kids were, but not like me. Not for the same reason. I'd gone funny about Mum again. Didn't want to let her out of my sight. Got so she'd stop on her way to the lavatory and call, 'Coming with me, Sand?' Sarky.

We both worried about Gran, though.

People weren't on the phone then, and with doodlebugs going off here there and everywhere, we'd no way of knowing whether they'd got her, so one day Mum decided it'd be best if she came to stay with us. She could have Joyce's bed. We set off to fetch her, but when we got there she wouldn't come. 'Old Adolf's been trying to get me out of here for four years!' she shouted. 'If I leave now, he'll think the war's starting to go his way.'

We laughed walking home, me and Mum. We didn't know it, but it was the last laugh we'd have for a long, long time.

Princes End Primary School
'Success for all'

Six

'Telegram, missus.'
Boy on a bike at the
kerb outside our
house.

'No,' says Mum
when he holds it out
to her.

You expected a telegram all the time in
the war but you didn't want it, hoped it'd
never come. So she's shaking her head and
he goes, 'Mrs Willoughby?'

'Yes,' she whispers, but she still won't have

it so I put my hand out. The boy looks at me. 'We're not supposed to . . .'

'It's all right,' I hear myself say. 'I'm her daughter, I'll see to it.' He puts it in my hand, murmurs sorry, moves off. I read the address on the flimsy yellow envelope. It's ours all right. Mum's at the door, fiddling with the key, trying to get it in the lock. Little mewing noises are coming from her and I realise she can't see the hole because she's crying. 'Give it here, Mum.' I take the key, open the door, steer her in with my hand on her elbow, shut the door.

'D'you want *me* to open it?' She'd peeled off her cardy and hung it on the banister. She shook her head, so I held out the envelope. She plucked it from my fingers, screwed it up, shoved it in her cardy pocket and set off towards the kitchen. I called after her, 'Mum, it's *got* to be opened.' She stopped, turned and gave me a look that'd stop a clock. I fished in the hanging cardy and held out the crumpled telegram, trying not to burst into tears. 'Come on, Mum, you can take it.' It was a slogan from the Blitz: *we can take it*. She snatched the thing out of my hand, smoothed it, tore it open.

It was Joyce. A flying bomb had fallen on the battery, killing the entire crew. My sister was dead.

I can't describe the hours after that. Don't want to. Mum's screams were so loud Mrs Ashcroft came dashing round, thought we were being murdered. She was an angel, that woman. An angel flying low the way she got Mum sat down, fetched her tea, rocked her, sat with her all through that first night. *I* wouldn't have known what to do. She had to go home next morning,

family of her own, and after that it was up to me.

I don't know how I managed to change so completely in the space of a couple of days, but I did. I suppose it was *having* to. I mean, I'm not kidding, Mum was like a baby. Couldn't feed herself, dress herself, keep herself clean. Sat in the chair for hours on end, weeping. It was *me* thought of sending Dad a telegram about Joyce. He might not come but I thought he'd a right to know. I must've gone a bit crazy because I kept thinking, Joyce'll be here soon, *she*'ll know what to do. Then I'd remember and burst out crying.

I shopped, cooked, cleaned. It was good for me in a way because I hadn't time to worry about the doodlebugs, which continued to come over thick and fast. *Hundreds* of Londoners were being killed. Our guns had given over shooting at the flying bombs because if they *hit* one it'd fall on the houses just the same. The RAF sent fighter planes after them, and they sometimes managed to explode one in the air or make it fall in open country, but mostly they were getting through.

It got so my whole life was dragging Mum up and down the cellar steps, because she'd stopped caring whether she lived or died.

One day Mrs Ashcroft stopped me in the street as I staggered home with the rations. 'Would you like me to fetch your grandma, love?' she asked. 'It's a lot of responsibility for someone your age.' She looked dead worried. I smiled and shook my head.

'It's all right, Mrs Ashcroft, I can manage.' And the amazing thing is, it was *true*.

One thing bothered me though. It was a thought. A selfish thought I suppose, but I couldn't help it. What I kept thinking was, I don't count with Mum at all. She'll lean on my arm, let me hold a cup to her lips but it's as though I'm not really there. All she thinks about is Joyce and Dad, but *I'm* the one keeping her alive. It's me she depends on. Why can't she think about me once in a while? Like I said, a selfish thought which I managed to keep to myself.

There came a day, a strange warm day in

June when suddenly the street outside our house filled up with military vehicles, bumper to bumper. Lorries, jeeps, armoured cars, tanks. They rattled the windows, made the house vibrate. I'd settled Mum on the sofa and was getting ready to slip up the

shops when I noticed a change in her, something to do with the passing convoy. She was gazing out the window and, for the first time in ages, there was a light in her eyes. A gleam of interest. I looked at her.

'D'you want to come *with* me, Mum?' I asked. 'Get a better view outside.' I didn't really think she'd come, but she nodded. My heart soared as I helped her on with a cardy.

The kerbs were lined with people watching the vehicles, waving and smiling at the soldiers perched on them. The soldiers were British and American. Some people started laughing and I stood on tiptoe to see what they were laughing at. It was an American armoured car with a message scrawled on it. *No leave, no babies.* I didn't get it. What I *did* get, and I think Mum got it too, was a feeling that this mass movement of troops signalled something important. Something *big*. It was a feeling which made you *vibrate*, like the houses. Mum didn't say anything, but there was fire in her eyes. I practically had to *drag* her to the shops, and we'd just set off back when we heard the familiar buzz of a doodlebug. We couldn't get across to the public shelter because of the convoy, so I pulled her close to the camouflaged flank of an armoured car and told her to crouch down. We didn't see the flying bomb but we heard it pass over, and moments later there was the usual bang. We straightened up and walked on, and when we turned the last corner we saw that the house had gone.

Seven

Mum collapsed. One whimper and gone, crumpled on the pavement. I thought she'd died. Dropped on my knees in a drift of broken glass, shaking her shoulder, going, 'Mum, Mum, oh Mum, don't you leave me too.'

People standing about, gawping. After a bit a policeman shoved me aside, laid his head on her chest. 'She'll mend,' he says. 'That your house, love? Well, there you go then – fainted from the shock I expect.'

He loosened her blouse and fanned her

with a ration-book and she came to. Somebody fetched a cup of tea and a chair and in five minutes she was sitting up and taking notice, only she'd lost the spark of animation that'd got her out the house. Two WVSs showed up, wanted us to go to the

community centre, but I said no, I'm taking her to Gran's. We were halfway there, Mum leaning on my arm, crying, when I remembered I'd forgotten to thank the lady for the tea.

So Gran took us in. Funny it should happen that way round after we'd planned on having her with *us*. She wept for hours when we told her about Joyce but I think it helped Mum, being with *her* mum. Things weren't much easier for me, though. Gran had arthritis – my Arthur, she called it – so she couldn't get about much. I found myself shopping and cooking for three instead of two, *and* getting them both down the cellar steps every time a doodlebug went over.

This went on day after day, night after

night. I think I got *past* sleep – stopped needing it, what with listening for that detested noise and getting my two invalids in and out of bed in the blackout. How long I would have kept it up I'll never know, because it came to an abrupt end one Wednesday dinner-time when Gran's famous stew and dumplings were nearly ready.

We *must* have heard its engine, or . . . I dunno, maybe we'd heard so many we'd stopped being *able* to hear 'em. At any rate we were all three busy getting ready to eat and its motor cut out, and when it hit the ground eleven seconds later I was carrying plates to the table, Gran was stirring the pot and Mum was topping up the salt-cellar. There was a flash like the end of the world,

the windows came in and the fist of an invisible giant slammed into my back so that I flew across the kitchen and smacked face-first into the cellarhead door. I wasn't knocked out, I felt myself sliding down, saw the smear of blood I was leaving like a slugtrail. When I reached the floor, falling in slow motion, it was shaking. I lay on my back watching things slide off the Welsh dresser, hearing them smash. I remember thinking I ought to jump up, position myself to catch Gran's precious china as it fell. Then I decided that with floor and windows gone and probably the roof too, the china wasn't all that important. I think I might even have giggled.

All of this can't have lasted more than a

second or two, then I smelled smoke and saw flame and realised the place was on fire. I got up pretty quick then, I can tell you.

There was so much smoke I couldn't see Mum or Gran. I'd never have run out on them, not after all we'd come through, but I was feeling groggy and the smoke was making me choke and then I saw somebody beside me and it was Dad.

'Come on, sweetheart,' he says. 'Let's get you out of here.' And he takes my hand and we're walking towards the light. It didn't seem real. I remember thinking, *I must have died*. He left me standing in a shaft of sunlight and everything was blurred and I thought, *I've gone to heaven*, and then I saw Joyce and knew that I had.

Eight

Turned out I wasn't in heaven, but I did wind up in hospital. Dad was real, he rescued Mum and Gran. And Joyce wasn't dead, there'd been a right old mix-up there. Seems she'd swapped shifts with another girl, which wasn't allowed. They'd swapped identity cards and discs in case either of 'em was challenged. On the night of the doodlebug, this other girl was on instead of Joyce, and when they recovered the body with Joyce's ID they assumed it was my sister. In the meantime an off-duty ATS had

48

told Joyce her crew had been wiped out, and she'd collapsed, hysterical, knowing it should have been her. They'd carted her off to sick-bay, given her knockout-drops and identified her by the discs round her neck as Lucy Cornwell, which was the other girl's name. Of course the girls in Joyce's hut knew about the swap, but by the time they got up the courage to go to the CO, the telegram had been sent. He dashed another off telling us Joyce was alive, but it was never delivered because when the telegram boy got to where the house should be, there was just a hole in the ground. Dad had gone there too of course but, unlike the telegram boy, he knew where we'd be, and had reached Gran's in the nick of time.

Oh yes, before I forget. The reason we
didn't hear the doodlebug coming was
because it *wasn't* a doodlebug, but a V2.
The V2 was a rocket with a bomb in its
nose. It flew faster than the speed of sound

so you couldn't see it coming, and you didn't hear the noise of its approach till *after* the explosion. I didn't think there could be *anything* more frightening than a doodlebug, but the V2 was. There was no defence against it. It looked as though old Hitler was going to destroy London after all.

It never happened, and I'll tell you why. Remember all those lorries, tanks and armoured cars? Well, they were off to join the Allied invasion force which had landed in France on 6th June 1944. By September they'd over-run most of the V1 and V2 launch-sites. Doodlebug and rocket raids became fewer and farther between, then stopped altogether. They'd killed more than seven thousand people, so you can bet we didn't miss 'em.

Anything else? Oh, yes. Dad didn't go back to Stranraer, and he never saw the Canadian nurse again. He was at a bomber base somewhere in Norfolk till the war ended, then he came home to us. Joyce didn't go back to Banbury either. They said she'd had a breakdown and invalided her out of the ATS. I was glad, and Mum was too. The war in Europe ended on 8th May 1945. It was a Tuesday, and I was twelve.

Glossary

ATS (page sixteen)
Auxiliary Territorial Service – women's branch of the British army.

Blackout (page fifteen)
No street lights, all windows covered at night, vehicle headlamps dimmed. This was to avoid assisting enemy bombers in finding their targets.

Blitz (page fifteen)
Short for *Blitzkrieg* – 'lightning war'. Bombing by German aircraft.

Cushy number (page seventeen)

Easy job.

Doodlebug (page one)

The V1 – *Vergeltungswaffe* 1 – a pilotless aircraft or flying bomb. *Vergeltungswaffe* means 'vengeance weapon'.

Duffers (page seven)

Losers.

Jerry (page seventeen)

The Germans.

Morrison shelter (page nineteen)

A bomb-shelter resembling a steel dinner-table. Panels of wire-mesh enclosed the space under the table, forming a cage in which its owners sat during raids. Usually sited in house cellars, it was supposedly capable of withstanding the weight of a collapsing house.

Old Adolf (page twenty-six)

Hitler, the Nazi dictator.

Shrapnel (page thirteen)

Metal fragments from bombs and anti-aircraft shells.

Urchins (page seven)

Scruffy kids, often street kids.

WVS (page forty-one)

Women's Voluntary Service – now Women's Royal Voluntary Service.

If you enjoyed this
Mammoth Read try:

Roger's War

Robert Swindells
Illustrated by Kim Palmer

World War II has brought glamour to
Roger's village. Pilots of the US Air Force
are based there: Roger's heroes!

All of his life he has dreamed of being
special, of being like them. But Roger will
never know glory. He's dim,
everybody says so.

When Roger's wits are put to the test, can
he avert danger? Could the actions of a
few minutes really change his life forever?